Hi there,

I'm David Warner, Australian cricketer, and I'm really excited to introduce you to my new series of kids' books called **The Kaboom Kid.**

Little Davey Warner is 'the Kaboom Kid', a cricket-mad eleven-year-old who wants to play cricket with his mates every minute of the day, just like I did as a kid.

Davey gets into all sorts of scrapes with his friends, but mainly he has a great time playing cricket for his cricket club, the Sandhill Sluggers, and helping them win lots of matches.

If you're into cricket, and I know you are, then you will love these books. Enjoy *The Kaboom Kid*.

David Warner

Playing Up

DAVID WARNER

with J.S. BLACK, Illustrated by JULES FABER

SIMON & SCHUSTER
AUSTRALIA

THE KABOOM KID – PLAYING UP
First published in Australia in 2014 by
Simon & Schuster (Australia) Pty Limited
Suite 19A, Level 1, 450 Miller Street, Cammeray, NSW 2062

10 9 8 7 6 5 4 3 2 1

Sydney New York London Toronto New Delhi
Visit our website at www.simonandschuster.com.au

National Library of Australia Cataloguing-in-Publication entry
Author: Warner, David Andrew author.
Title: The kaboom kid: playing up/
                 David Warner and J. S. Black.
ISBN: 9781925030808 (paperback)
                 9781925030815 (ebook)
Target Audience: Upper primary school students.
Subjects: Warner, David Andrew.
                 Cricket – Australia – Juvenile literature.
                 Cricket players – Australia – Juvenile literature.
                 Cricket – Batting – Juvenile literature.
Other Authors: Black, J. S., author.
Dewey Number: 796.3580994

Cover design by Hannah Janzen
Cover and internal illustrations by Jules Faber
Inside cover photograph of adult David Warner © Quinn Rooney/Getty Images
Typeset by Midland Typesetters, Australia
Printed and bound in China by RR Donnelley

CONTENTS

FOR STEVE

CHAPTER 1

SIX AND OUT STEVE

Davey Warner gripped the worn red cricket ball in his hand. His thumb traced the rough seam in the cracked leather before he found the right grip. He gave his shoulders a stretch and jogged lightly on the spot.

'Game on,' Davey said quietly to himself.

As if responding to Davey's comment, the batsman at the other end of the pitch tapped the crease with the end of his bat and waited. His expression was of fierce concentration.

Davey found his mark and turned. 'Let's see how you like this one,' he muttered.

He came in a few paces off a short run and released his leg-break. But it pitched short of a length and a loud 'whack!' sounded. Davey watched as the ball sailed over his head to the outer.

What a cracker! Davey's dog Max yelped and then tore off after the ball.

'Stink!' Davey pulled a face.

Davey's older brother, Steve, looked far too pleased with his shot. 'You need to mix it up

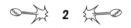

more,' he said to Davey. 'Try one that comes straight on.'

'Yeah, yeah,' Davey muttered.

It was Sunday afternoon and even though Davey had already played two games of cricket that weekend he was keen for more. Only trouble was, Steve was hitting him to all parts of the backyard *and* kept giving him unasked-for coaching tips. It was driving Davey bonkers.

Max loved nothing more than fielding for the Warner brothers. He'd retrieve ball after ball relentlessly, dropping it each time at Davey's feet in a slobbery pile.

'Hurry up, Max,' Davey called. He was itching to get his brother out.

Max let out a series of excited whines as he searched frantically through the overgrown shrubbery alongside the back fence.

'I can see how you're holding the ball, so I know how you're going to bowl,' Steve told Davey as they wandered over to help Max in his search. 'You want to keep the ball hidden from the batter.'

'Der, I know!' Davey had just about heard enough of Steve's advice.

Steve shrugged and said nothing. He was fourteen and captain of the Sandhill Saints. Davey knew that Steve loved cricket just as much as he did, but Steve didn't always love playing with his little brother. The feeling was mutual – Davey preferred to play cricket with his friends Sunil, Kevin and George. For one thing, they didn't tell him what to do.

Steve found the ball and after giving it a quick rub to remove most of the slobber he tossed it to Davey. They went back to their positions and Max moved to silly mid-on and crouched low. *You won't get it past me this time*, he seemed to say.

Davey ran in, trying hard to hide his grip. It felt awkward and he served up a full toss that Steve hooked to the fence for four.

'Double stink!' he cursed.

'Don't lose it, Davey,' Steve called when he saw the dark look on Davey's face. 'You can't just rely on your batting. You need to be able to bowl as well.'

'Yes, oh Great One.' Davey rolled his eyes. 'You aren't exactly Shane Warne yourself.'

He jogged over to the side fence that separated their house from his best friend Sunil's. Davey had lost count of how many runs Steve would have scored over the last hour.

Davey lined up at the end of his run-up for the next ball and tried to clear his head, but just as he was about to let rip his brother interrupted him again.

'Concentrate on line and length,' Steve shouted.

Davey slowed down and focused on controlling his delivery.

'That's too short,' Steve said, smacking it to the off side.

Davey tried again.

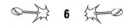

'That's too full,' Steve said, driving it back over Davey's head.

Max raced for the ball *again* with a delighted yap. He hadn't seen so much action in years!

'I'd concentrate on your spinners, if I were you,' Steve said as Davey approached.

'I'd put a sock in it if I were you.' Davey bowled the next ball as fast as he could but it was over-pitched, and Steve sent it flying over the fence.

'Great shot!' Steve threw his bat into the air.

But his delight was interrupted by a high-pitched squeal followed by a loud crash and the sound of something shattering.

'Davey Warner!' Sunil's mum shouted from the other side of the fence.

Davey pulled a face. 'Sorry, Mrs Deep!' he called. 'Look what you've done!' he hissed at Steve.

He jogged over to where Kaboom, his cricket bat, lay on the grass, waiting. 'Six and out. My turn to bat.'

But Steve was already wandering towards the house. 'I've got to meet Danny and Jerome for practice. 'We've got the big game against Shimmer Bay Skiffs on Saturday.'

'No way!' Davey shouted, holding up Kaboom. *My turn to bat!'*

'See you later, little brother.' Steve ruffled Davey's hair when he walked past him.

'David?' Mrs Deep was peering over the fence. She waved a broom in the air. 'I'm waiting!'

'Steve!' Davey called again, but his brother had already gone. *Typical.*

'Coming, Mrs Deep!' he called. At least he wouldn't have to hear any more of Steve's 'advice'.

Davey looked at Max. 'You stay here,' he said. But the dog was already dashing down the side path ahead of him.

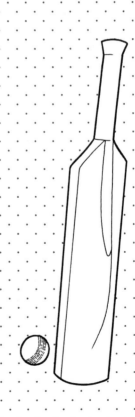

CHAPTER 2

ROUND ONE TO MUDGE

Davey gazed out of the classroom window at the dusty playing fields. He squirmed restlessly on the hard wooden seat. It was a brilliantly still summer's day – perfect conditions for cricket. In fact, it was perfect conditions for anything *other* than listening to grumpy old Mr Mudge drone on relentlessly with algebra questions while Davey's whole class – 6M, for 'Mudge' – nodded off.

'A boat is travelling at a constant speed for five hours, covering a total distance of 338.49 kilometres. How fast was it going?' Mudge asked in a monotone.

This is torture, Davey thought. *Does he really expect anyone to answer?*

Davey's mind drifted off to cricket, and he pictured himself at the crease, leaning into his bat, Kaboom. The ball came fast and straight. The crowd 'Ooh-ed' when they realised the ball was rocketing straight for his face, but he didn't even flinch. Judging it perfectly, Davey struck it and with a mighty crack sent it flying high over square leg and then the boundary for six.

The crowd erupted! 'Warner! Warner!' they chanted, cheering their hero.

Davey nodded and smiled, soaking up the adulation. Cricket glory, fans, playing for a rep side – it was all within his reach. Davey and his bat Kaboom were going places.

'Warner!' a familiar, cranky voice snapped Davey out of his daydream. '*What* is so amusing?'

Davey came back to earth with a painful thud. Mr Mudge's face was just centimetres from his own. The teacher didn't look happy, and his ears, which peeked out from under lank wisps of grey hair, were rapidly turning a shocking pink.

Davey remembered – maths. 'Yes, Sir?' he asked innocently.

'We're waiting for the answer, Warner,' Mudge drawled.

The answer? Davey didn't even know the question. Something to do with a boat? He looked at the board for clues but it was just a mass of squiggles and equations. He made a show of studying his notes, but the page in front of him was full of cricket bat designs.

Mudge crossed his arms impatiently. 'We're waiting.'

Just as Davey opened his mouth, there was a knock at the classroom door.

'Saved by the bell, Warner.' Mudge scowled at Davey. 'Don't move a muscle. I'll be back.'

The school principal was standing in the doorway.

Mudge gave her a welcoming smile. 'Lavinia – I mean, Mrs Trundle! What can I do for you?' He hurried over to join her and they were soon deep in conversation.

'Phew!' Davey stretched out his legs in front of him.

Davey still had sore muscles from a weekend of cricket. His foot kicked his backpack, which was on the floor in front of him. Davey knew that sticking out of his bag was his cricket bat, Kaboom. It was his lucky bat and had been signed by two of his heroes, Ricky Ponting and Shane Warne. The signatures were important to Davey – if he was in a tight spot on the field, he would think of his heroes and it would help him find his focus.

Davey's hands itched to touch the willow. He glanced at Mudge. Davey could have sworn he saw him blush, although it was hard to tell, because the teacher's ears had changed back from shocking pink to just pink.

Mudge was still laughing and talking to Mrs Trundle. Davey could hear snatches of conversation about, *yawn,* lawn bowls and, *double yawn,* class grading.

Davey pulled out his bat and held it in his hands.

'Hi, Kaboom,' Davey said quietly.

Kaboom was made from beautifully balanced English willow. Davey had put on his own grip and he oiled the bat carefully at the start of the season, giving the face and edges extra care and attention. It was well worn in now, especially since it had so many dents and cherries from hitting sixes out of the park.

The call to play was bigger than Davey, and he just couldn't help himself. He slipped out of his seat and adopted a stance at the crease, demonstrating one of his favourite shots, the square cut.

He looked around at his friends Sunil, George and Kevin, who were each sitting in different corners of the room, specifically so they couldn't talk about cricket all day. 'This is how Ricky would deal with a short ball outside the off stump,' Davey whispered rather loudly.

Sunil scrunched up a piece of paper into a tight ball and pitched it across the room to Davey.

Every other student in 6M watched in silent awe as the paper ball flew high into the air. It seemed to move in slow motion as it bounced off the top of Mudge's balding head and landed on the floor beside him.

Davey sucked in a breath. *Uh-oh!*

'Now you've done it,' said Bella Ferosi, the school captain who sat next to Davey. Her brown ponytail flicked back and forth as she looked from Mudge to the soon-to-be-shark-bait Warner.

'Warrr-nerrr!' If Mudge had been blushing before, he now looked set to blow a fuse. His ears had gone purple, and crimson red blotches had appeared all over his face.

'You're dead meat, Shorty.' Mo Clouter sat on Davey's other side and was perhaps Davey's least-favourite person.

Mrs Trundle's eye twitched. Davey knew that meant she was about to lose it. Clearly unimpressed, she quickly took her leave, but not before throwing Mudge a look that could have killed a cat.

Mudge turned on Davey. 'When I get my hands on you, Warr-nerrr . . .' he spluttered and tiny sparks shot out of his ears.

Davey held Kaboom out in front of him in mock defence.

'Give it here.' Mudge reached a hand out for the bat.

'Ah, this is my lucky charm, Sir,' Davey said. 'I can't play cricket without it.'

'GIVE IT TO ME!' Mudge spat out the words with such force that little bobbles of spit flew from his mouth and landed on Davey's shirt.

'Please, Sir! I'll do detention, anything . . .' Davey pleaded.

'The bat!' Mudge grabbed hold of Kaboom and pulled.

But Davey couldn't let go. It wasn't that he was a show-off, but Kaboom was his most prized possession. Together, Davey and his bat had plans. They'd made a pact to not only win the season but to show the selectors the art of batting and that they had a place on the rep side.

Mr Mudge didn't see it quite the same way. 'Let it go,' he seethed.

There was a short and vicious tug of war before Davey finally gave up. Mudge cleared his throat, smoothed a strand of oily hair over his scalp and placed the bat on his desk with a clunk that made Davey wince.

George, Kevin and Sunil gave Davey looks of sympathy.

'How long will you have it, Sir?' Davey asked meekly as he sat down.

'Not sure, Warner,' Mudge said. 'Long enough.'

Mo sniggered. 'You gonna cry now, Shorty?'

Davey slid down low in his seat. He hated to admit it, but for once the boneheaded bully was right. He did feel like crying.

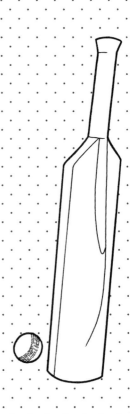

CHAPTER 3

NO KABOOM GLOOM

'I can't believe I've been out-Mudged by Mudge,' Davey said glumly.

Davey opened his lunchbox, stared at the contents and replaced the lid. He was usually starving by lunchtime, but today he was too churned up about Kaboom to eat.

'He's really got you by the goolies,' Sunil agreed, crunching on an apple. He dug in his bag and held another one out to Davey, who shook his head.

George, Sunil, Kevin and Davey were eating lunch in their usual spot near the row of oleanders which lined the school playgrounds. It meant they could eat and then get back to playing cricket, which was how they usually spent their lunch hours – rain, hail or shine.

'How long do you reckon Mudge'll keep Kaboom?' Davey asked.

'He confiscated Anh Nguyen's trick yo-yo for six months,' George said.

'And he still has Luca Panas's game cards,' Sunil added.

'So, like forever?' Davey groaned. 'That's the rest of the season!'

He fell back on the grass and closed his eyes. Then he remembered. 'We've got training this arvo.' He sat up abruptly. 'What am I going to do?'

'You can borrow my bat,' George said.

'Thanks, Pepi.' Davey sighed. He appreciated the offer, but no bat in the world could replace Kaboom. Davey knew the bat so well it was like an extension of his own body. It was as if Mudge had cut off his left arm.

'I got a bad case of the Mo Clouter blues,' Kevin murmured.

Davey looked up to see Mo and his friends, Nero and Tony, approaching. The best way Davey had found to deal with the meatheads was to ignore them. Davey lay back down on the grass and closed his eyes. Before too long, Mo's hulk of a body blocked out the sun and Davey was cast into shadow.

'Oi, Shorty . . .' Mo looked down at Davey. 'What'll you do without your *lucky bat,* you poor little peanut?'

'You losing sleep over me, Mo?' Davey asked, with his eyes still closed. 'I never knew you cared.'

'Not likely,' Mo retorted. 'I never think about you cricket kooks.'

'You don't think, period,' Davey shot back at Mo.

'You'll never see your bat again!' sneered Mo.

'What would you know?' Davey replied.

'Mudge took my lucky cap a year ago and never gave it back,' Mo said bitterly.

'Thanks for the intel.'

Mo pulled a face when he saw what George was eating. 'Urgh!'

'Want one?' George offered up a lunchbox full of neatly wrapped vine leaves.

'No way!' Mo backed away. 'Freaky foreign food! Come on, boys, something smells off here.'

The hulk and his cronies ambled off.

'And we were having such a great chat,' Sunil called after them, giving them a friendly wave.

'Mo's right,' Davey said. 'Mudge will never give Kaboom back willingly. He hates cricket. He'd be loving this.'

'What can you do?' Kevin asked.

'I have to get it back myself. Whatever the punishment, I don't care. Kaboom is mine and Mudge has no business taking away my stuff.'

'Go, Warner!' Sunil said, clearly impressed.

'Where do you think he'll keep it?' Davey asked his friends.

'Staffroom?' Sunil suggested.

'Classroom?' Kevin added.

'Sports room?' George said, through a mouth full of food.

'We just have to keep looking,' Davey said. 'I'm getting Kaboom back, if it's the last thing I do!'

When Davey made up his mind about something, he stuck to it.

CHAPTER 4

MUDGE MAKEOVER

Mudge made a point of leaving Kaboom
lying on top of his desk for the rest of the day.
Confiscating Davey's bat seemed to have given
the teacher a new lease of life. He talked non-
stop all afternoon with something close to
enthusiasm.

Mo had long since drifted off, but the rest of the class were in a state of panic. Enthusiastic Mudge was even *worse* than normal Mudge. The man would just not shut up.

Davey sighed and scratched his head.

Even Bella Ferosi, who was not only school captain but 6M's most diligent student, appeared to be having trouble keeping up with Mudge as she furiously scribbled down notes.

Sunil had had enough. He shot up a hand.

'Yes, Sunil?' Mudge looked a little peeved at being interrupted.

'Uh, Sir, the bell went ten minutes ago.' Sunil smiled so that his dimple showed. 'I'd be happy to stay, but I have to get to coaching college.'

Davey rolled his eyes at his friend's ability to suck up, and Sunil shot him a sly grin.

'Look at that!' Mudge exclaimed, glancing at the clock. 'Yes, of course, Deep. Mustn't hold you kids up from your extracurricular activities!'

He dabbed at the layer of sweat on his forehead and chuckled to himself.

Kids? Davey mouthed. Mudge never called them *kids*. Monsters, abominations probably, but not kids. And he *never* agreed with them.

'Off you go, then!' Mudge called after them, with something close to affection. Who had taken Mudge away and replaced him with this imposter? Davey wondered.

Davey hung back as the rest of 6M filed out of the classroom. Sunil's fib had given Davey an idea. He'd tell Mudge that the bat belonged to his Uncle Vernon.

'Um, Sir . . .'

'No, David,' Mudge replied, without looking around while he wiped down the board. 'I have *not* changed my mind.'

'But—'

'If you take one step out of line, I'll call your mother and tell her what happened today. I'm sure she'll find it *interesting*.' Mudge hummed as he pottered around the room, tidying up.

Mmm. Not so good. Davey changed plan. 'Do you know where you'll be keeping it, Sir?' he asked casually.

Mudge turned to him and gave a wink. 'THAT is the million-dollar question, isn't it, Warner? For me to know and you to find out.'

Davey knew it was useless to argue. He abandoned the classroom and made his way over to get his bike. His mates would already be down at the beach having a hit before training.

At the bike racks, Davey found Mo, Nero and Tony blocking his way.

'Oh dear, Warner,' Mo pouted like a toddler having a tantrum. 'What are you going to do without your p-p-p-precious bat?'

Davey gritted his teeth and unlocked his bike. There was no point biting back. Anyway, he'd had enough for the day. First Mudge, and now Mo.

'Going home to have a cry?' Mo taunted.

Davey paused. There were a few comebacks lining up in his head, but it would just infuriate Mo, possibly to the point of no return. *Time to dig deep*, he thought.

He looked at Mo and gave him his biggest grin. 'Not at all. I couldn't be happier, Clouter.'

Then he jumped on his bike and pedalled away without looking back.

Later, at training, Davey was unsure where to begin without Kaboom. He hung back as the others sorted themselves into positions and began to practise. Their coach Benny hadn't arrived, but that wasn't unusual. Benny *showing up* to training would be more unusual.

'Want to use my bat?' Sunil offered. He had a beautiful Kookaburra bat that he polished obsessively.

Davey knew it was a big thing for Sunil to lend his bat to anyone. But Davey shook his head. It wasn't the same.

'Nah, I'll bowl.' He grabbed his ball from his school bag and headed to the other wicket. 'Steve, the know-it-all cricket oracle, reckons I need the practice, anyway.'

'Let's see what you've got then, Warner,' Sunil said. He grabbed his bat and took up his position at the crease.

Davey gave the ball a quick rub against his thigh. He might as well take Steve's advice and concentrate on his leg-spinners. He couldn't always rely on his batting – especially now he was Kaboomless. *Being a better bowler will make me a better batter,* he told himself.

As Davey did a few arm warm-ups, Steve's advice kept coming back to him: *Concentrate on getting the ball to the right place.* But legspinners were really difficult to get right.

After a few warm-up bowls, Davey was still finding it hard to get the ball in the right spot. He bowled to George next, but it was too short and George pulled it square. The next ball was too full and wide and George smacked it through the off side.

'Come on, Warner!' George called out. 'Give us a hard one!'

Finally Davey landed the ball in the right spot. It turned and beat George, knocking over his off stump.

'Ah!' That felt a little better.

'Way to go!' Sunil shouted.

'Over here, boys!' Benny was standing on the edge of the park, bags of equipment at his feet.

'Only half an hour late,' George said to the others. 'Not bad for Benny.'

The boys wandered over. Benny was puffed from lugging all the gear a good two metres from his car.

'Sorry I'm late,' he said, scratching his scalp. Davey watched as white flakes tumbled onto his shoulders and rested there in a snowy patch.

While the team gathered around him, Benny took a moment to catch his breath. 'I've got some news,' he announced, a quiver of excitement in his voice.

Davey's ears pricked up. He caught Sunil's eye. He also looked as if he was eager to hear what Benny had to say.

'I've been given a heads-up that a regional selector is keen to come along this week to take a look at you all,' Benny said.

'Yes!' Davey punched the air. It was the news they'd been waiting for all season.

'That's awesome!' George said.

'Don't get your hopes up,' Benny added quickly, with a look of commiseration. 'The chances of any of you lot getting picked are pretty close to zero. It's always best to aim low in my experience,' he concluded, farting at the same time.

Despite the pong, the team immediately broke into excited chatter. Even Benny's usual

pessimism couldn't take the shine off the news. A selector coming to watch them meant that they were on the lookout for new talent for the local rep side. It was the moment Davey had been waiting for. The news was huge.

'When will he be here?' Sunil asked.

'Tomorrow night,' Benny continued, 'so we'll do an extra training night this week. Make sure you're all on time,' he said, waggling a sausage finger at them.

That was rich coming from Benny, thought Davey. The last time he turned up on time was probably 1985.

'This is my chance!' Sunil sucked in his breath, his eyes glassy with excitement.

'Dream on, Deep,' George said. 'It's me they'll want.'

Sunil rolled his eyes. 'Only if they need someone to do the drinks run. Then you'd be a shoo-in.'

George silenced his friend with a look.

Mudge couldn't have picked a worse week to ruin Davey's life. Without Kaboom, what hope did he have for impressing anybody?

'Boys, we need a plan.' Davey drew the others in close to him. 'I've got to have Kaboom back in time for tomorrow night. Otherwise I'm cactus.'

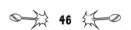

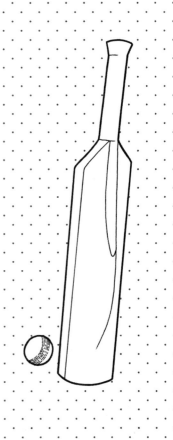

CHAPTER 5

FACING THE MUSIC

It was dark by the time Davey wheeled his bike up the side path. He crossed his fingers and prayed that Mr Mudge hadn't called his mum to tell her about the bat. If Mudge *had* told her, Davey would be in BIG trouble – so much trouble, in fact, that he might as well turn around and leave home, never to return.

Davey knew his mum would freak if she found out that Kaboom had been confiscated – for two reasons. The first was, well . . . Davey could hear her now: *You were playing cricket in class? And Mr Mudge got hit in the head! What were you thinking?*

The second reason was that the bat had been a very special birthday present from his parents and granddad. If his mum found out, she'd think he didn't know how to look after his stuff. *Looks like we won't be buying you any more serious presents like that again,* she'd say. And even worse: *Granddad's very disappointed!*

Max appeared around the corner and tore down the path towards him, barking and wagging his tail furiously.

'Max, you're a menace,' Davey said, giving the dog a rough scratch behind the ears.

Pushing past his dog, he wheeled his bike around the back and looked up at the house. All seemed quiet, but then, that didn't mean anything.

'Is Mum home?'

Max cocked his head. *You'll find out*, he seemed to say. He wasn't giving anything away. After all, Davey's mum fed him!

'Mmm.' Davey got the hint. 'No cracking you, Mr Mutt,' he said. 'All right, where's the ball?'

At the mention of the word 'ball', Max jumped up on his hind legs and did a little dance.

'Here you go.' Davey pulled a ball from his bag and pelted it to the far end of the yard.

Max took off at lightning speed. He launched himself at the rolling ball, grabbed it in his teeth, turned a one-eighty and charged back towards Davey.

It was a perfectly timed routine. Just as Davey bent down to pick up the ball, Max dropped the slobbery article at his feet.

'Let's see what you think about this one!' Davey took a run-up and came hurtling towards Max.

'Mix it up, keep it on a length . . .' he said, mimicking his brother, before firing a googly at the imaginary batsman.

Max yelped in admiration and raced after the ball.

'Not bad,' said a voice.

Davey swung around in surprise.

Steve was slouched against the frame of the back door. 'Dinner's ready,' he said.

Davey climbed the back stairs. 'Is Mum home?'

'Yep,' Steve said. 'She cooked it.'

Davey dropped his voice so his mum wouldn't overhear. 'I'm in a bit of trouble,' he whispered to Steve. 'I was mucking around and, well, Kaboom got confiscated.'

'Let me guess . . . Mudge?' Steve laughed.

Davey nodded.

'Mum'll *freak*!' Steve exclaimed a little too loudly.

'Shh!'

'I won't dob, if that's what you're worried about.'

'Boys, dinner's ready!' their mum called.

'Do you think she knows?' Davey asked. He peered anxiously through the open door, trying to get a glimpse of the expression on his mother's face.

Steve shrugged. 'Better get inside.'

'Hang on . . .' Davey said. 'Can I use your bat?'

'Mate, no way!' Steve held up his hands in protest. 'We've got the game against the Skiffs this weekend, and practice is on every night.'

'I forgot about that,' Davey mumbled, disappointed.

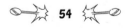

'Anyway, you should practise with lots of different bats. You shouldn't just rely on one.' Steve was giving advice *again*.

'Quit it, will you?' Davey snapped. 'I don't want other bats. I want my bat!'

'Down, boy!' Steve backed away. 'Cool it.'

'Benny says a selector might turn up tomorrow night,' Davey muttered.

'Seriously?' Steve asked. 'Well, it's still good advice. You don't want to be scared in a game just 'cause you don't have the perfect equipment. You've got to mix it up.'

'Scared? I'm not *scared* of anything!' Davey had heard enough of Steve's advice to last until the year 2065.

'David and Steven Warner!' their mum shouted in a shrill voice. 'For the last time, DINNER IS READY!'

The boys looked at each other in alarm.

Davey grimaced. 'Well, apart from Mum sometimes . . .'

The two brothers hurried inside.

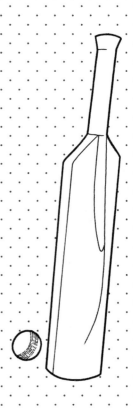

CHAPTER 6

CAUGHT OUT

'I've never been at school this early before,'
Kevin said as they entered the school grounds.
There were only one or two students on the
near-empty playgrounds. 'It's like a ghost
town.'

'McKinley's always early,' Sunil said, 'and lucky for you blokes she *lurves* me.' He flashed his best dimpled smile.

After Benny's announcement, Sunil had done some fast thinking and come up with a plan for them to find Mudge's hiding place for Davey's bat.

'*Please*,' Davey said, 'just lead the way, lady-killer.'

'Watch and learn.' Sunil smirked as they approached the admin office.

Operation Kaboom was a go.

Sunil approached the desk of Mrs McKinley, Head of Administration, while the others waited just inside the doorway. McKinley wore coke-bottle thick glasses and was so old that nobody at school remembered a time when she hadn't worked there. Despite looking a little like a bilby, she wasn't a bad old stick.

Sunil cleared his throat. 'Good morning, Mrs McKinley!' he said brightly.

'Is that you, Mr Deep?' Mrs McKinley leant forward and peered at Sunil through her glasses.

'Yes!' Sunil smiled so his dimple showed. 'Mr Mudge has asked for another forty copies of the band excursion form, please.'

Mrs McKinley shook her head and waggled a finger. 'That Mr Mudge! He does keep me busy.'

'Don't I know it!' Sunil joked.

Davey felt a teensy bit bad about hoodwinking McKinley. She might be ancient, but she was always kind.

'I know that one.' Mrs McKinley shuffled off in slow motion to find the file. 'Pink, if I remember correctly.'

'Thank you,' Sunil crooned.

She licked a finger and selected a piece of pink paper from the top of the pile. 'All right, dear.' She shuffled off down the hall. 'I'll just copy them for you.'

Sunil waited until she was out of sight.

'Now!' Sunil whispered.

Davey, George and Kevin sprang into action. They scuttled past the office and down the corridor as Sunil joined them.

'That should buy us a few minutes,' Davey said, patting Sunil on the back.

The four boys crept towards the green door at the end of the corridor. The staffroom was strictly off limits to students. Nobody they knew had EVER tried to enter it without permission and lived to tell the tale.

Davey's mouth felt dry as Kevin cautiously opened the door a crack. He noticed Kevin's hand was shaking.

Kevin peered inside. 'All clear,' he said and entered the room. The others followed close behind.

The staffroom was brightly lit, with fluorescent light shining on every desk surface. Around the sink area there were dog-eared signs about washing up on the wall and reminders about rosters. But a quick look around the room revealed no Kaboom in sight.

'Cupboards!' Davey moved at lightning speed across the room and began to open the built-ins that lined one wall. They scoured every available storage area, but all they found were odd mugs, plates and cake platters.

'Zilch,' George said.

'We'd better get out of here.' Sunil glanced at the clock on the wall, 'McKinley's not *that* slow.'

Davey was disappointed, but he nodded.

'Er, guys . . .' George pointed to the door.

The door handle was turning. Davey looked around for somewhere to hide, but there was nowhere. On impulse, he bobbed down behind a table and pulled Sunil down with him.

'I know you're in here,' said a familiar voice as the door opened. It was Mudge.

'Holy moly.' George sucked in his breath. 'We're done for.'

Mudge glared at them. Gone was the jolly teacher from the day before. Back was the cranky teacher they knew so well.

'What do we have here? The staffroom is OUT OF BOUNDS for students!' Mudge thundered, entering the room and stopping in front of Davey and Sunil. Davey studied his long white socks and hairy knobbly knees. He stood up slowly.

'There's a really good explanation for this, S-S-Sir,' Davey stammered. His mind raced. He was so dead they may as well have buried him right there.

'I'm all ears, Warner.' Mudge was seething. His ears had gone such a dark shade of purple they were almost black.

'My bat, Sir . . . The selector . . .' Davey's voice trailed off.

'Yes?' Mudge snapped. 'All I hear about is this bat, bat, bat! One of the things that annoys me most about cricket is the confounded bat!'

'Sir, I need it to play,' Davey tried again to explain.

'Warr-ner, you will be lucky if you *ever* see your stupid cricket bat again!'

Davey's eyes widened in horror. He was speechless.

'It's just . . . please, Mr Mudge,' Sunil pleaded, 'there's a selector coming to our cricket practice tonight. It's a big deal.'

'Could you just give me my bat back for the night?' Davey asked, his eyes wide. 'And then you can lock it up.'

Mudge's eyes narrowed, and his cheeks grew more and more crimson.

'I'm sorry, boys, but you're confusing me with someone who CARES!' he exploded.

The boys stared at the floor in silence.

'AND I'll be calling your mother now to tell her that your bat will be in my possession for some time,' Mudge added with satisfaction.

'No!' Davey cried.

'No?' Mudge raised an eyebrow.

'Sir,' Davey mumbled.

Mudge rocked back and forth on his loafers. 'Now you lot can join me for rubbish duty for the, let's see—' He made a show of pondering. 'I think before school and lunchtime for the rest of the term ought to do it!' He grinned.

'But—'

'No buts, Warner!' Mudge stomped a clumpy foot for emphasis. 'Now, *scoot*!'

'Sir,' each of the boys mumbled as they filed past their teacher.

'I think Mrs McKinley wants a word with you all,' Mudge added, as he frog-marched them out of the staffroom. 'For some reason, she has forty extra band forms photocopied for me. You wouldn't know anything about that, would you, Deep?'

Sunil shook his head and made his way down to the office to face the music.

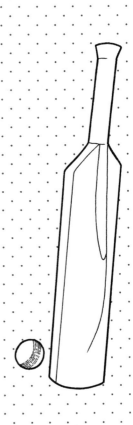

CHAPTER 7

SELECTOR REJECTOR

That night, George, Davey and Sunil gathered with the rest of the Sandhill Sluggers for the extra training session at Flatter Park. As yet there was no sign of Benny, or the so-called selector.

Davey was anxious. They all were – a mixed concoction of nerves and excitement.

Davey decided to take Steve's advice. He needed to try using other bats and improve his batting that way. He had no Kaboom, so he might as well use the next best thing.

'Can I change my mind and try your bat, Deep?' he said to Sunil.

'Thought you'd never ask!' Sunil pulled his Kookaburra out of his kit. It was a heavier bat than Kaboom, and to Davey the weight and balance felt completely different. He ran his hand down the length of the bat, getting to know it. Like Kaboom, it had a history of the games Sunil had played imprinted in dents and marks along the willow.

Davey took a swing at an imaginary ball. It felt strange to him, so he adjusted his grip on the handle and swung again. This time he overbalanced and nearly fell.

'Get a grip, Warner!' he muttered to himself. 'This is embarrassing!'

Davey got George to give him a few throw downs, to get the feel and see if he could find the sweet spot. Then he walked out to the crease and tried to find a stance that felt just right.

'Ready?' Sunil called from the bowler's end.

'Born ready,' Davey quipped as he moved into position.

Davey and Sunil had been playing cricket together for years and knew each other's tricks. But for the first time in a long time Davey felt unsure of himself as a batter. But he wasn't going to let Sunil know that.

Sunil ran in fast and Davey saw the tell-tale flick of his wrist. He shifted his position for the speed of the ball, but felt slow and clumsy. Sunil's fast ball seemed to fizz off the pitch and Davey just managed to jam his bat down and keep it out.

'Nice one!' Sunil shouted.

It had been a complete fluke, but it gave Davey a little boost of confidence. The bat felt so alien that he needed to change almost everything about the way he played.

'I'll get you this time,' Sunil said.

'I'm shaking, Deep,' Davey replied. He nodded to Sunil to let him know he was ready. He lined himself up and focused on positive thinking. *Just think about the ball*, he told himself.

'Prepare to eat dirt,' Sunil called out.

Sunil was on fire. He surprised Davey with another fast yorker and Davey played right over it. It cannoned into his stumps, clean bowling him.

'What the . . . ?' Davey was dazed. The ball had sizzled straight past him and he'd been too slow to even react.

'HOWZAT?!' Sunil exclaimed as he sprinted around in tight circles.

'Great ball, Sunil!' Ivy called from third slip.

Davey shook his head. He just wasn't himself. Instead, he was doing a great impersonation of how to play cricket badly.

Sunil commiserated. 'Sorry, Warner,' he said, giving his friend a slap on the back.

Davey shrugged. 'It was a great ball.'

'Well bowled, Sunil,' said Benny, who had just joined them in the middle. He turned to the man with him and added, 'He's not usually so good.'

Davey realised that Benny had arrived while they were playing and had been watching with another man – the selector. Trust Benny to turn up just as he got smashed!

'This is Rob, the selector I mentioned,' Benny said.

Davey's stomach lurched. Of all the plays for the selector to see, that would have to be the worst. Any hint of confidence Davey had got back drained away.

Benny's mobile rang as he was about to introduce Rob to each player. 'Hang on a mo, got to take this.' He wandered off, chatting into his phone.

Rob said hello to the team with a smile and they gathered around him while he scribbled a few notes on a small notepad. There was silence as they all watched him with bated breath. Rob finished writing and scanned their expectant faces.

'Nice to meet you,' Rob said, stepping forward to shake Sunil's hand. He shook all the players' hands in turn but didn't give Davey a second glance. His eyes were fixed on Sunil.

'A yorker is a hard ball to pull off,' Rob said. 'If you get it right, it can beat almost any batter.'

'Thanks,' Sunil said. He couldn't wipe the smile off his face.

Rob glanced at Davey momentarily. Davey felt his face grow hot and flush with embarrassment.

'There's probably nobody here you'd be interested in,' Benny said, then belched. He had finished his phone call and joined them again. 'The team tries hard, but let's face it, we're not very good.' Benny hoicked up his pants. Despite his round belly, Benny was a compulsive Harry Highpants.

Rob checked his watch and shook his head. 'I've seen enough thanks, Benny.' He turned to Sunil. 'Can I get your name and a phone number for your parents?' He had his notebook at the ready. 'I'd like to give them a call to have a chat about the possibility of you playing for the rep team.'

Sunil spelt out his name and gave Rob his parents' mobile numbers. 'This is my friend, Davey Warner,' he then said, stepping to the side to introduce the selector to Davey.

Rob smiled politely and fell into conversation, asking Sunil about his cricket aspirations. Davey felt like a fish out of water.

The selector hadn't even noticed him. The worst thing about it was that Davey understood why. If he was a regional selector, he wouldn't have noticed himself either. Davey was even more determined to get Kaboom back and show the selector just what he was made of.

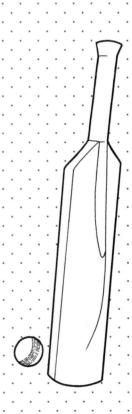

CHAPTER 8

SNIFFER DOG SUCCESS

Davey woke with a start. It was dark outside, but he could have sworn he'd heard a noise outside his bedroom window.

He glanced at Max, who was fast asleep on Davey's bed, back legs in the air, snoring lightly.

'Some guard dog you make!' Davey nudged the dog, who rolled over and promptly went back to sleep.

Davey hopped out of bed and opened the curtains.

'Yikes!' Davey nearly fell over backwards at the sight of Sunil's face pressed right up against the window.

'Scared the life out of me,' Davey muttered.

Sunil mouthed the words '*Open up*' and held a finger to his lips. *Sunil must be up to one of his schemes*, Davey thought. He wondered what it was.

He opened the window and peered sleepily at his friend. 'It's not time for morning detention yet, is it?' Davey asked.

'I've had an idea about where Kaboom might be,' Sunil said. 'I'll tell you on the way to get Kevin and George.'

Despite being grounded *forever* for getting his bat confiscated, Davey nodded and began dressing.

'We'll need one of your shirts,' Sunil added, 'and the smellier the better.'

'Easy!' Davey handed over his training shirt from the night before. It ponged all right.

'And we need Max,' Sunil said.

Davey gave a low whistle and Max leapt to his feet. He stood alert on the bed, tail wagging, ready for action. Davey climbed out the window and joined his friend.

'Come on, dog,' Davey called to Max.

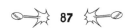

Max leapt expertly out of the window and Sunil closed it quietly behind him.

George did a sweep of the empty playground with his binoculars, taking in the surrounding quadrangle of buildings.

'The coast is clear,' he reported.

'That's because nobody in their right minds would be at school this early,' Kevin grunted.

'There's Trundle!' Kevin pointed towards the east corner of the school. 'Right on time, as usual.'

Mrs Trundle insisted on unlocking all of the classrooms in the school each morning. After completing this task, she monitored the main school gate – trying to catch out any uniform offences and generally being a nuisance.

The sound of keys jangling grew louder. Max's ears pricked up, but Kevin shot him a dirty look, willing him not to bark. For once, Max did what someone wanted him to do.

Kevin watched as Mrs Trundle unlocked the 6M classroom door.

'We've got about ten minutes before Mudge arrives for detention,' Sunil said.

The boys shot inside the classroom. They knew exactly where to look. Mudge had a large metal cabinet in which he stored a treasure trove of confiscated items.

'Check it out,' Davey said, holding up Duncan Carver's water pistol.

Sunil found Luca Panas's game cards and Mariana Larkin's comic books.

'I know that hat!' Kevin picked up an old battered footy cap.

'It's Mo's,' Sunil said.

Kevin shook off the dust and punched the cap back into shape.

'Correction,' he said with a cheeky grin, as he put the cap firmly on his head. '*Was* Mo's.'

Sunil laughed. 'I'd like to say it suits you, but Mo isn't known for his good taste.'

Max barked his agreement.

The boys rifled through all the stuff, but didn't find the cricket bat.

George opened Mudge's desk drawers and a small leather-bound book caught his eye. He picked it up and scanned the pages.

'Mudge writes poetry.'

Davey looked over George's shoulder at the book. It was love poetry. A name caught Davey's eye. Lavinia. The name Lavinia was repeated on almost every page. Lavinia? Did that mean Trundle?

An image of Mudge and Trundle kissing popped into Davey's head. 'Urgh!' he exclaimed and immediately stopped reading.

'You're up, Max.' Sunil gave the dog a scratch. Max sat on his haunches, eager to take part in the adventure. Sunil held Davey's shirt out for Max.

'Take a good whiff of Pong de Warner,' he instructed the dog.

Max obliged by taking a good sniff and wagging his tail. He jumped up on his hind legs and did his dance. *I know that smell!* he seemed to say.

'That's right, Max,' Sunil said encouragingly. 'We need you to find Davey's bat.'

Max ran around in circles and let out a series of short sharp barks. He jumped on Davey.

'Sshh, dog!' Davey hissed. 'Not me, the bat!'

Max tilted his head and froze. He had a whiff of something. He jumped down and began following his nose, zig-zagging around the room. He came to a tall coat cupboard in the corner and scratched at the door.

'He's got something!' Kevin exclaimed.

'Bingo!' Davey said.

George hastily shoved the notebook into his back pocket and joined the others. The boys clamoured to open the cupboard. Inside were three black umbrellas and a pale blue duffel bag with a wooden handle sticking out one side.

'Kaboom!' exclaimed Davey.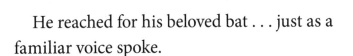

He reached for his beloved bat . . . just as a familiar voice spoke.

'I see you've found your bat, Warner,' Mudge said in barely more than a whisper. He stood planted in the open doorway, his magenta ears illuminated against the early morning light like a pair of wings about to take flight.

'Y-yes, S-Sir,' Davey stammered.

Mudge came over to the cupboard and slammed the door shut, narrowly missing Davey's fingers.

'Don't worry . . . I'll find a new hiding place for it,' he told them.

'Sir!' Davey said, crestfallen.

Mudge looked like the cat who'd eaten the cream. 'Your detention just got extended by another term!' He glared at Max. 'And how many times do I have to say GET THAT DOG OUT OF HERE!?'

They had been so close, but it looked like operation Kaboom was a no-go.

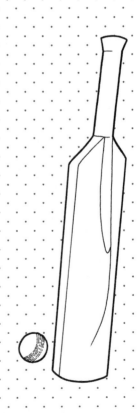

CHAPTER 9

A HAT-TRICK

The morning couldn't go quickly enough for Davey. Mudge lorded it over him by dangling Kaboom before his eyes. By the time the bell rang for lunch, Davey was desperate.

This can't be happening, he said to himself when he joined the others outside the classroom.

He didn't have Kaboom and every minute of his life was taken up with Mudge, Mudge, Mudge.

'You lot better be waiting when I get back,' Mudge threatened as he went to the staffroom to get a coffee. He'd given them ten minutes to eat their lunch before rubbish pick-up duty began.

Kevin put on a battered old peaked cap.

'What's with the non-regulation headgear?' Davey asked.

'Only Mo Clouter's most prized possession,' Kevin explained with glee.

'Does he know yet?' Sunil asked.

'Any minute now.' Kevin nodded in the direction of the quadrangle. Mo and his entourage were approaching.

 98

'Like my new hat, Clouter?' Kevin called.

It took a moment for Mo to register what Kevin was talking about. After all, his brain did run at a slower speed than most. Then his pimply face erupted in a scowl. He wasn't happy.

'You punk, that's my hat!' he yelled. He raced over to where Kevin stood.

'Correction. *My* hat now.'

Mo lunged at Kevin, but was too slow for Kevin's fast fielding reflexes. With lightning feet, Kevin darted to one side and easily dodged Mo's outstretched hand.

'You're going down!' Mo thundered.

'Over here!' Kevin taunted Mo by tipping his cap at him and scurrying in circles around him.

Mo was lunging at him over and over again. He kept missing by a fraction.

'Look, that's my lucky hat!' Mo growled. 'Give it here!'

'Have to catch me first,' Kevin said, sprinting away.

Mo growled and lumbered after Kevin, chasing him around the quad. After five rounds, Mo bent over and paused to get his breath back.

'What's wrong, Mo?' Davey asked.

Mo straightened up and shook a fist at Davey.

'I'll get it back, don't you worry,' Mo snarled.

'If you say so,' Davey shot back, smiling.

Mo's face had turned purple. He was absolutely livid with rage. 'You'd better keep an eye out – all of you!' he sputtered.

He took off after Kevin again, but it was useless – Kevin was far too fast for him.

Sunil and George had tears in their eyes they were laughing so hard. But Davey had other thoughts on his mind besides Mo. As far as he was concerned, Mudge had declared war in the same way that Mo had. It was game on.

He was even more determined to get his bat back. The question was, where would Mudge hide it next?

CHAPTER 10

THE BIG SWINDLE

Davey, Sunil, George and Kevin had arrived at school early again.

The idea to look in the school sports store room had been Davey's. 'The perfect place to hide a bat is among heaps of other cricket bats,' he said.

'It's worth a shot,' George agreed.

But when they got there, the door to the store room was locked firmly with a large rusty padlock.

Davey gave it a tug, but the padlock held fast. 'So much for that idea,' he said with a sigh.

Sunil wandered around looking for a way in, but there was only one small window covered by metal bars. 'The toilets are part of the same building,' he said. 'Could we get in through them?'

Davey shrugged. 'Let's check it out.'

They went into the boys' toilets. There was a small window high above the sink that led directly into the storage room.

'You're a genius!' George gave Sunil a friendly punch.

'Better believe it,' Sunil agreed.

George studied the small opening. 'Reckon you could squeeze through?' He looked at Davey.

Davey nodded.

'I'll hoist you up.' George bent his knees and locked his hands together. Davey put one foot on George's hands and his friend gave him a lift.

'Oof!' George was rewarded with a knee in the mouth.

'Woah!' Davey wavered wildly but managed to steady himself. He reached for the ledge. 'Got it!'

'Hurry up! You're heavier than I thought,' George muttered.

'Nearly there,' Davey said through gritted teeth. He opened the tiny window a little further and, with some effort, managed to squeeze his head and his shoulders through the small opening. He was about to pull himself through, when . . .

'Someone's coming,' George hissed. 'Quick! Jump down!'

Davey tried to back out, but his shoulders were held fast. 'I can't!' he groaned. 'I'm stuck.'

He was neatly wedged in the small opening, head and shoulders on one side and his bottom and legs on the other.

'HEY!' a loud voice boomed from the doorway. 'What's going on in there?'

George, Sunil and Kevin froze as heavy footsteps echoed on the cold cement floor. Mo's ugly mug appeared around the corner. He burst out laughing.

'You should see your faces, or in your case, Shorty, your bum!' He pulled a face. 'Ooh, no! Did you think I was a teacher?'

'What do you want, Clouter?' George asked.

'I want my hat back,' Mo said with a sneer.

'Guys . . .' Davey said, 'I'm stuck.'

'I'm here to make a trade.' Mo held up a duffel bag. 'Shorty's hunk of wood for my lucky hat.'

'Where'd you find it?' George asked with suspicion. 'Mudge moved it.'

'Look, do you want it or not?' Mo sounded impatient. He dangled the bag in front of them.

'Guys,' Davey called, 'get me down!'

'Hang on,' Sunil said. He reached for the duffel bag.

'Uh uh.' Mo shook his head and held the bag just out of reach. 'Give me my hat first.'

Kevin narrowed his eyes. 'How do we know we can trust you?'

'What choice do you have? Your little friend can't play without it, can he?'

'Guys, I'll handle this,' Davey said. 'Just get me down!'

Kevin glanced at George and Sunil. They both nodded.

'All right.' Kevin held out the cap.

Mo grabbed it and put it on before dropping the duffel bag on the ground next to George. A slow smile appeared on Mo's face.

'GET ME DOWN!' Davey kicked his legs against the wall.

Sunil and Kevin each took one of Davey's legs and yanked him down.

He fell hard onto the cement floor. 'Ow!' Davey grimaced as he rubbed his shoulders.

There was silence as George unzipped the duffel bag.

'What?' Davey asked when he saw the look on George's face.

As soon as Davey saw the bat, he knew it wasn't Kaboom. With a sinking feeling, he watched George pull it out. It was ancient. Mo had probably paid fifty cents for it at a garage sale.

'You asked for it,' Mo growled.

'Where's Kaboom?' Davey was seething.

'You'll never get near it. Mudge carries it around with him all the time.' Mo leered and tipped his cap to Kevin. 'See you, suckers!' He sneered and ran off.

Davey hated to let Mo or Mudge get the better of him, but how was he ever going to get Kaboom back now?

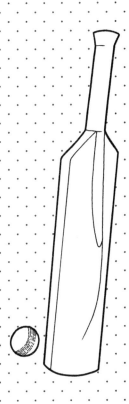

CHAPTER 11

BATTING FOR BRADMAN

Davey sat on the back steps staring into space. Usually Friday afternoon meant cricket with the boys, but being grounded meant he was stuck at home.

He absentmindedly gave a tennis ball a rub and turned it over in his hand. Max whined and nudged his nose up against Davey's leg, hoping he'd get the hint. The dog tucked his hind legs neatly underneath his tail and sat down. He gazed at his owner hopefully.

'Here, dog.' Davey chucked the ball across the lawn towards the back fence. He didn't even bother trying to bowl properly. His arm ached and his whole body felt heavy.

Max trotted back along the grass and dropped the wet ball at Davey's feet. He rolled it back and forth expertly with his nose and whimpered.

'No more, Max,' Davey said abruptly, then headed into the house.

Davey was rarely home this early. Normally he'd be out playing cricket with his friends until dinner time. Nobody else was home and the house felt spookily quiet.

He opened the pantry door and stared at the contents. Usually he was ravenous after school, but today nothing appealed. He closed the door and ambled into the TV room. A quick flick of the remote told him that nothing interested him.

Once inside his bedroom, Davey flopped on the bed with a sigh. He lay on his back and gazed up at the ceiling. One of the reasons he loved his bat so much was because it had been a gift from his granddad and they had spent time together sanding and oiling it to perfection. His granddad had taught him how to look after a bat – what the willow wanted and how to tell when it needed attention. He knew it would sound stupid to say out loud, but his bat was like family.

Above his bedhead was a poster of his hero, Ricky Ponting. The poster was so old and faded it had taken on a greenish tinge. Davey still loved looking at it, even if Sunil had drawn a beard on Ricky's chin and coloured in two of his teeth.

Now Davey flopped over to look at his hero. Davey could imagine Ricky yelling out to the bowler: 'Mate, is that all you've got?'

'Did you ever feel like giving up, Ricky?' Davey asked.

Ricky rearranged his cap and considered the question. *There were times when I doubted myself.*

'I know how you feel,' Davey said.

It's up to you to turn things around, Davey. Ricky looked directly at him. *Nobody else can do it for you.*

'How? I don't have my lucky bat!'

Don Bradman practised without a bat and look what he did! You have to improvise, Ricky continued. *Nothing ever goes the way you want under match conditions, either. You just have to be prepared!*

And with that, Ricky gave Davey a knowing wink.

Davey thought about Ricky's advice. His brother Steve and Ricky were both saying the same thing. Davey needed to take control. He needed to stop letting cricket haters like Mudge and Mo get in his way.

Suddenly, he felt energised. 'Max!' he yelled at the top of his voice.

Max jumped up onto the bed and licked his face.

'Urgh, gross!' Davey pushed Max off the bed and got up. 'Stop slacking off, Max, we need to practise!'

Davey searched inside one of the kitchen drawers. Ricky's tip about The Don had given him an idea. He found an old golf ball of his dad's and headed outside to the pitch. Then he pulled up one of the wickets and carried it over to the side of the house.

When Steve got home half an hour later, Davey was still practising his batting using a wooden stump and hitting a golf ball repeatedly against the wall. Steve smiled and headed inside the house.

CHAPTER 12

BIG BROTHER

It was finally Saturday morning. Davey and Sunil were in Davey's backyard having a hit. For once there was no Sluggers game, because they had a bye, but Davey was fired up to practise his leg-spin bowling. It still wasn't going well.

'I need to rip the ball more to make it spin and bounce,' Davey said. 'But it's really hard.'

Sunil was no great shakes as a batter, but he was having no problem dealing with Davey's gentle leggies, especially as Davey couldn't maintain a consistent length.

'Yeah, you should bowl more often!' Sunil agreed. 'I've never batted so well!' With that, he gave Max another four to retrieve.

'It's only spinning one way,' Davey said, thinking out loud. 'I'm going to have to learn to bowl a wrong'un like Shane Warne.'

'You've got to do something, Warner,' Sunil said with a grin, ''cause this is just too easy.'

Davey made a Mo Clouter face. 'You could live to regret those words!'

'Watch me,' Sunil retorted, waiting. 'Let's face it, you have the ugliest bowling action I've ever seen!'

Davey went back to his mark. He gripped the ball tightly, came in off his short run and ripped the ball as hard as he could. It pitched just outside leg stump. For once it bounced and spun viciously.

'Take that!'

Sunil was beaten. He pushed forward and only succeeded in edging the ball to where first slip would normally stand. Max had been waiting at mid-off and collected the ball between his jaws before dropping it back to Davey.

'Hmmf,' Sunil said.

'I've still got it!' Davey gloated.

'I bet you can't do that again,' Sunil said.

'Bet you I can!'

Davey was getting his groove back. As he walked back to his mark, he noticed Steve coming out of the house. He was wearing his cricket whites.

Max let out a happy yap and raced over to Steve.

'No more advice, bro!' Davey said, bristling. 'I'm doing everything you told me.'

Steve laughed. 'Good! Because we need you.'

'Who needs me?'

'The Sandhill Saints,' Steve said. 'We've got the big game against Shimmer Bay Skiffs.'

Davey had forgotten about Steve's big game. He would give anything to watch it and support Steve, even if he was the world's most annoying older brother.

'Have you forgotten, I'm grounded, for . . . like, *ever*,' Davey said.

'You can come,' Steve said. 'I cleared it with Mum.'

'You did?' Davey was taken aback. This was news.

'We need an eleventh man,' Steve explained. 'Lee Woon's injured.'

'You want *me*?' Davey was floored.

Steve dug his index finger into Davey's chest. 'We want you.'

'Way to go, Warner!' Sunil slapped his mate on the back.

Davey was taken aback. 'I thought . . . I thought you didn't think I was any good.'

'You're *okay*,' Steve said with a grin. 'Not bad for an eleven-year-old.'

'High praise from the master!' Davey did a mock bow.

'Don't let it go to your head,' Steve warned.

Davey beamed. He was still stunned at the news. Playing for the under-fourteens. That was massive! His mind raced.

'Hurry up and grab your stuff,' Steve said. 'Game starts in an hour. Danny's mum is going to pick us up in about ten minutes.'

Steve headed back inside, leaving the two friends staring at each other.

'Lucky you, Warner,' Sunil said. 'You never know, that selector could be there to watch.'

Davey remained rooted to the spot. He stared at Sunil dumbfounded. As soon as Steve was out of earshot, he gripped Sunil by the shoulders.

'It's a total disaster,' Davey said, shaking him. His voice sounded full of fear. 'This is an emergency! I need Kaboom and I need it *now*!'

CHAPTER 13

BAT OR NO BAT

Davey and Sunil took off at breakneck speed down Eel Avenue to Kevin's place. They didn't have much time.

Kevin's dad answered the door. 'Kevin and George are still asleep, but feel free to wake them up,' he said with a grin.

George had slept over at Kevin's after staying up to watch Australia play India on TV. Kevin was snoring gently, his mouth hanging open. A thin trickle of drool had created a wet patch on his pillow. Sunil wanted to take a photo with his phone, but there was no time. George was curled up on a mattress on the floor.

'McNab!' Sunil shook his friend roughly. 'Pepi! Wake up!'

'What?' Kevin's eyes shot open in fright. He sat up and hastily wiped his mouth.

'Urgh!' George groaned as Davey nudged him with his foot.

'Davey needs help,' Sunil said. He grabbed some clothes from the floor and threw them at Kevin.

'Why?' Kevin asked as a pair of boxers hit him in the head. He pulled a face.

'I'm playing for the under-fourteens!'

'That's great!' George sat up.

'No it's not!' Sunil snapped. 'Have you seen how big they are? Davey's going to get eaten alive.'

'That's going a bit far,' Davey said drily.

'If we don't help him get back Kaboom, there could be nothing left of him by the time this game is over.' Sunil was pacing up and down the room.

Davey shot him a withering look. None of this was helping his confidence.

'You saw Mudge on Friday,' Kevin reminded them. 'He didn't let Kaboom out of his sight.'

'So,' Sunil concluded, 'wherever he is today, he'll have Kaboom with him!'

'Mudge plays lawn bowls at Penguin Palace RSL on Saturdays.' Kevin winked knowledgeably.

'We could go and plead with him,' Sunil suggested.

'He's not going to give us Kaboom!' Davey was running out of time. 'Mudge hates cricket even more than he hates me.'

George didn't say anything. He was deep in thought. 'We have to think more like Clouter,' he said finally.

Sunil made a face. '*Clouter*?'

'Mo didn't have Kaboom, but he offered us a trade and we took the bait,' George explained.

'Hook, line and sinker,' Davey muttered.

A car horn beeped outside.

'Thanks for trying, guys but it's no use.' Davey shrugged. 'I've got to go.'

'Wait!' Sunil grabbed his Kookaburra from his bag and handed it to his friend. 'You might need this.'

'Thanks, Deep.' Davey took the bat and left.

'Good luck!' his friends called after him.

Davey's stomach was in knots as they pulled
up at the Shimmer Bay cricket ground. A large
crowd of supporters had already gathered.

'Just in time,' Steve said. The umpires were
already on the field.

They grabbed their gear and tumbled out of
the car. Davey recognised a few people.
His dad was sitting with a group of other
fathers up in the stand. Howie gave Davey
a wave.

'Go, Davey!' His dad gave him a big
thumbs-up.

Davey waved back furiously and nearly
whacked a Shimmer Bay player in the head
with his elbow.

The player ducked just in time. 'Watch out!' he snapped.

Davey swung around to apologise and found himself face to face with Josh Jarrett, also known as Mr Perfect, the best cricket player Davey knew and the captain of the Sluggers' rivals, the Shimmer Bay Juniors.

'What are you doing here?' Davey asked.

'I could ask you the same question,' Josh said, looking amused. 'I sometimes sub for the Skiffs.'

'Guess I'll see you out there, then,' Davey said.

'This is the big league, Warner.' Josh smiled. 'Better keep your eyes open or you might get hurt.'

Davey wasn't sure which made him more nervous – seeing Josh, the game ahead, or having no Kaboom.

But he had no more time to worry about it. It was time to play cricket.

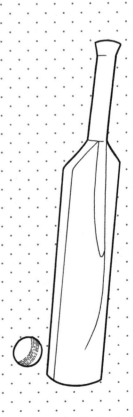

CHAPTER 14

THE BIG LEAGUE

The Shimmer Bay Skiffs won the toss and opted to bat first. Steve gathered the team together for a quick pep talk. Davey knew that, as captain, Steve would have to be on the go continuously, thinking on his feet and making it up as he went along. It was a huge job and now he had his little brother to look after.

'Today's a big match,' Steve said. 'Let's get out there and smash these guys, they're nothing.'

'Well, technically, their current for-and-against record against us is seven to one,' Jerome piped up. 'In their favour,' he added, a little unnecessarily.

'Yeah, but they don't play with heart like we do,' Steve countered with conviction.

'They've got seven rep players and the fastest bowler in the league,' Jerome pointed out.

'You can shut up now, Jerome.' Steve silenced his friend with a meaningful look.

Jerome shook his head, but stayed quiet.

'We've done the hard work,' Steve went on with enthusiasm. 'Just stay on form and do your best.'

The players nodded and wished each other a good game. Steve placed his fielders and saved Davey for last.

'You won't bowl today,' he told Davey. 'I'll get you to field at third slip.'

Davey nodded.

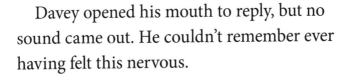

'You okay?' Steve asked.

Davey opened his mouth to reply, but no sound came out. He couldn't remember ever having felt this nervous.

'You can do it, Squirt,' Steve said. Then he added, 'Just don't mess up.'

As the opening batters approached the wickets, Davey took up his position.

His palms felt too wet and his mouth too dry. He stretched lightly on the spot, shifting his weight from one foot to the other, keeping his legs light and spry. It helped a little to have Steve's belief in him, but at the end of the day he was on his own.

Davey concentrated hard and tried to ignore the bowling ball in his stomach. He was going to do all he could to hold his own in the under-fourteens and, failing that, just stay alive.

The openers made a solid start, but off the fourth ball of the fifth over, Steve got one to duck away. The Skiffs' opening batter, Karesh, was drawn wide and his attempted drive only managed to get a thick edge. Davey flung himself to the right, stuck out his hand. He was as stunned as Karesh that he somehow managed to hold on to the edge. One wicket down.

'Not too shabby, bro!' Steve yelled. He ran over to give his brother a hug. Even Jerome gave Davey a nod of respect.

It was a start, but Shimmer Bay continued to bat well. Davey saw little action again until Josh came out as number four, at the fall of the next wicket. Davey was surprised that Josh batted so high in the order in this grade, and burned to get him out. Josh made a point of flashing Davey a big smile every time he scored a run – and that was too often. It was infuriating, but Davey grudgingly had to admit it – the guy could play.

Although he'd lost a couple of partners, Josh was batting really well and scoring quickly. With his own score on forty-six, he was shaping up to take the game away from them.

Then he edged one past the slips, down towards the third-man boundary. Davey chased from third slip with everything he had and more. He thought he might throw up from the effort, but ran hard all the way. He picked the ball up just inside the boundary, turned and threw in one motion. The return was right over the stumps and Danny the wicketkeeper took the bails off. Josh had been looking to keep the strike, but didn't make his ground. He was run out!

'I kept my eyes open that time,' Davey said with a big smile when Josh passed him on his way off the field.

'Warner . . .' Josh muttered as he left. He looked furious.

The lower-order batters for the Skiffs kept the runs going and, at the end of their twenty-five overs, they were eight down for 128 – a challenging total.

It was the Saints' turn to bat, chasing 129 runs to win.

They lost two early wickets, but Steve went in at number four and their captain was in good form. He helped them reach sixty-five with only four wickets down. Davey tried not to get too excited. If they kept going at this rate, they should win.

But you never knew how quickly the tide could turn. The Skiffs' fast bowler, Zane, came back into the attack for a few overs and caused a collapse. The Saints lost four wickets for very few runs.

Davey was next in. He was batting at number ten. He picked up Sunil's bat. It wasn't Kaboom, but it was the closest thing he had.

'Go, Davey!' his dad shouted. Davey's stomach did another flip and he concentrated on taking deep breaths as he approached the pitch.

Steve was the other batter. The situation was dire. They had enough overs left, but still needed fifty-nine runs to win, with only two wickets standing.

'Try to give me all the strike and I'll get the runs,' Steve advised. 'You just have to stick around and grind this out.'

'I'll grind *you* out,' Davey said firmly. 'Put a sock in it, Steve.'

Steve glared at his young brother. 'I'm the captain and your job is just to defend,' he said.

They had a small chance of winning this game, if they didn't kill each other first.

The first ball Davey faced was a swinging yorker. He managed to jam his bat down on it and it squirted off to the leg side for one. Steve drove the next ball to the boundary for a four.

They pressed on. Little by little the target was reduced. Davey began to relax a little and started to time his shots better.

We can do this, Davey realised. *We could actually win!*

Although Zane peppered Davey with short and fast deliveries, he had made thirteen runs. *An unlucky number for* some, *but not me*, thought Davey.

Josh came on to bowl and over-pitched his first delivery. With a rush of confidence,

Davey instinctively knew what to do. He stepped down the wicket and drove the ball long and high over the bowler's head for four. The crowd loved it!

Josh glared at Davey.

'So much for getting hurt,' Davey said smugly.

Steve walked down the pitch and Davey thought he was coming to congratulate him on the shot. 'What was that?' his brother snapped.

'A great shot?' Davey felt on top of the world. 'A legend in my own lunchtime?'

'A loser who doesn't listen,' Steve hissed.

The two brothers glared at each other.

'Forget your history with Josh,' Steve said. 'I said *play it safe*! Protect your wicket, DO YOU UNDERSTAND?'

Davey couldn't believe it. How dare Steve bawl him out in front of everyone when he was playing so well?

Who did Steve think he was? Davey thought bitterly as Steve stalked back to his end. He thought he could yell at Davey just because he was his little brother. It was so unfair!

Davey sneaked a look at the scoreboard and the team watching from the sidelines. They looked grim. He could just make out Jerome and Danny glaring at him. With a jolt, Davey realised Steve was right. He'd been thinking about himself and not the whole team.

Realising the seriousness of the situation, Davey concentrated on protecting his wicket while letting Steve score most of the runs. He deflected the next delivery off his hip for a single, to put Steve back on strike.

'Good one, Davey.' Steve praised his efforts.

The brothers communicated well and finally began to work together as a team. They managed to put on fifty runs together. While Davey's contribution was only seventeen, it was much needed. They were getting very close to the target.

With nine runs still needed to win, the Skiffs' best fast bowler, Zane, came back into the attack for his last over. Steve cut the first ball for four, but going for a big shot on the next ball, he was caught behind. That was it. He was out.

This time he didn't give Davey any advice as he walked off the pitch. Davey kind of wished he had.

The fate of the game rested with Davey and the Sandhill Saints' number eleven.

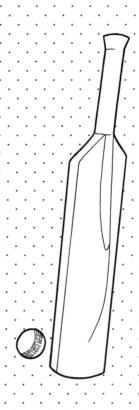

CHAPTER 15

POETRY IN MOTION

With just five runs still needed to win the game, out walked Harry, the number eleven batter. Harry was a great bowler but a well-known bunny. He'd do almost anything to get out of batting and the whole team supported him in this wish. It was harsh but true – Harry was the world's worst batter.

Davey met Harry mid-pitch. He noticed that Harry was carrying two bats.

'Your mates thought you might need this,' Harry said, handing a bat to Davey.

Davey took the bat and looked at it in surprise. It was Kaboom! Davey had never been so pleased to see a piece of wood in his life.

'What the . . . ?' Davey looked up at the stand and saw Kevin, George and Sunil with his dad. So the boys had made it to the game. And they'd brought Kaboom? Davey couldn't get his head around it. How did they get Kaboom away from Mudge?

'Forget about the bat, Davey,' Harry said. 'The team's stuck with an eleven-year-old and me. It's not looking pretty.'

'That's where you're wrong, Harry,' Davey said. He held Kaboom to his chest and felt a surge of confidence. 'This is a game changer. We can win this!'

'O-kay . . .' Harry looked doubtful. 'What's the plan?'

'We need five runs, right?'

Harry nodded. 'Yeah, I checked with the scorer.'

'Just try and block the first one somehow or let the ball hit you,' Davey said. 'No matter what happens, *run*. I'll be coming.'

'I'll do my best,' Harry said.

Harry moved back to his crease to face his first ball. He looked really nervous and Davey watched anxiously as Zane sent down one of his fastest balls. Harry never had any hope of actually hitting the ball with his bat, but he bravely took it on the arm.

'Oof!' Harry grimaced as the ball made contact.

'Ooh,' cried the crowd in sympathy.

'Run!' Harry yelled, taking off from his end.

Davey took off and sprinted down the pitch with all his might. They just made it, scampering through for a leg bye.

Only four runs to go! Zane didn't look happy. He went back to the top of his mark and glared at Davey.

'This'll sort the men from the boys,' he said loudly enough for Davey to hear.

'If you thought that one hurt, wait till you feel this!'

Davey glanced at Harry, who was still rubbing his arm. He shut him out. Davey ignored Zane and his sledging and he thought about Ricky and everything he'd learned. He gripped Kaboom. All other distractions faded away. It was Davey, Kaboom and the ball.

'You'll feel it all right,' Davey said to himself, as his eyes followed Zane's every move.

Zane ran in and let fly a fast bouncer aimed straight at Davey's head.

'Ooh!' the Saints supporters voiced their alarm when they saw the trajectory of the ball.

Up until now Davey had tried to avoid hitting the short ball, ducking and weaving and concentrating on keeping his wicket. As the red blur came screaming towards him, Davey realised there would be no second chances. It was now or never. He had Kaboom back in his grip. He didn't even have to think about how to stand or hold his bat. It felt completely natural. It was time to take action.

'Show me what you've got, Kaboom,' Davey said. He kept his eyes fixed on the ball and swivelled on his left foot. Kaboom hooked the bouncer high and handsome, way over the fine leg boundary for a huge six!

They'd won! The crowd erupted in a roar and Davey felt completely stunned.

'We did it!' Harry yelled, running down the pitch towards him. He looked completely and utterly ecstatic.

It took a minute to sink in. They'd won. They'd won! Davey was suddenly surrounded by people jostling him, slapping him on the back.

As usual at the end of a game, the players from the two teams all shook hands with each other before leaving the field. Josh even managed a grudging 'Good shot, Warner', before joining his team to talk over their defeat.

Even Steve was beside himself. 'Well played, Davey,' he said, grabbing his brother in a bear hug. 'You little beauty!'

Rob, the selector, appeared at Davey's side, his little notebook in his hand. 'You played some impressive cricket today, Warner,' he said. 'I'll be keeping an eye on you.'

'Thanks!' Davey couldn't remember ever feeling so happy. He hugged Kaboom and ran to find his friends.

Later that night Sunil, George, Kevin and Davey were hoeing into homemade pizzas at Davey's house.

'I still don't understand how you got Mudge to give Kaboom back,' Davey said.

George chuckled. 'The poetry book. When we got sprung in the classroom, I stuck it in my pocket. I'd forgotten I still had it.'

'Urgh!' Davey pulled a face. 'Trundle and Mudge – so gross!' It was enough to turn him off his pizza. 'But what's that got to do with Kaboom?'

'I had to give Mudge something to keep him quiet. We sneaked into Penguin Palace RSL and found Mudge's bag. Sure enough, there was Kaboom. Remember he was taking it with him everywhere? So we took Kaboom, but we left Mudge his book.'

'So he'd know to keep quiet or we'd spill about his little crush!' Davey exclaimed. 'That's gold!'

George nodded smugly. 'I tell you one thing,' he said, before taking another bite of pizza and munching happily. 'I won't be doing rubbish pick-up for a long time!'

'Cheers to that!' Kevin agreed.

The friends clinked their glasses of lemonade. There was a day–night game of cricket on TV to watch and they had plenty to celebrate.

Just then they heard a loud cry from the kitchen.

'Max, you thieving mongrel!' A split second later, Max flew into the room past the boys with a whole salami gripped in his teeth. Max and Davey locked eyes for an instant before Max pinned his ears back and flattened himself under the couch.

'Have you seen Max?' Davey's mum appeared in the doorway, her apron covered in flour and pasta sauce. She was brandishing a wooden rolling pin.

George, Sunil and Kevin all looked at Davey.

'Sorry, Mum, he's not in here.'

'Hmm.' Davey's mum looked unconvinced, but after a quick glance around the room she stalked back to the kitchen. 'When I get my hands on that dog . . .'

Davey stuck his head under the couch. Max was gnawing enthusiastically on the sausage.

'Max, you're a mutt!' laughed Davey. 'But I'm glad someone else is in trouble with Mum for once!'